Perfect

Max Amato

Scholastic Press
New York

Published by Scholastic Press, an imprint of Scholastic Inc., *Publishers since 1920*. SCHOLASTIC, SCHOLASTIC PRESS, and associated logos are trademarks and/or registered trademarks of Scholastic Inc. The publisher does not have any control over and does not assume any responsibility for author or third-party websites or their content. No part of this publication may be reproduced, stored in a retrieval system, or transmitted in any form or by any means, electronic, mechanical, photocopying, recording, or otherwise, without written permission of the publisher. For information regarding permission, write to Scholastic Inc., Attention: Permissions Department, 557 Broadway, New York, NY 10012.

Library of Congress Cataloging-in-Publication Data

Names: Amato, Max, author. Title: Perfect / by Max Amato.
Description: First edition. | New York : Scholastic Press, 2019.
Summary: A fussy eraser tries to keep the pages perfectly clean
despite the scribbles of a mischievous pencil. | Identifiers:
LCCN 2018005708 (print) | ISBN 9780545829311 (hardcover)
Subjects: LCSH: Erasers—Juvenile fiction. | Pencils—Juvenile fiction.
Writing materials and instruments—Juvenile fiction. | CYAC:
Erasers—Fiction. | Pencils—Fiction. | LCGFT: Picture books.
Classification: LCC PZ7.1.A496 Pe 2019 (print) | DDC [E]—dc23

ISBN 978-0-545-82931-1

10 9 8 7 6 5 4 3 2 1   19 20 21 22 23

Printed in China 62

First edition, February 2019

The text was set in Mrs Eaves XL Serif.
The artwork for this book was created with photographs and
hand-drawn images collaged in Adobe Photoshop.
Book design by Max Amato

This page is perfectly clean.
Just the way I like it, and just the
way it's going to stay.

Squiggles be gone . . .

And smudges . . .

And you, too!

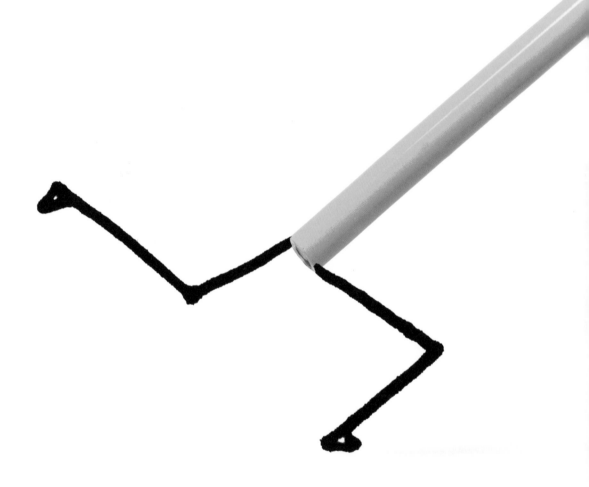

No pencil can mess with me.

Hey!

Get back here!

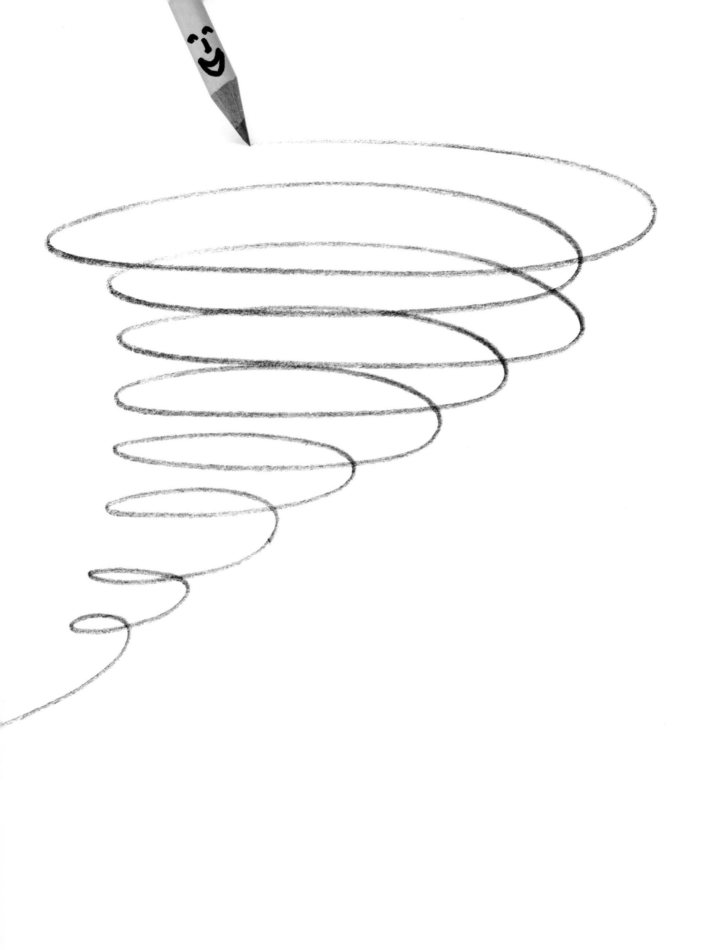

Look at this mess!
It's everywhere!

Seriously . . .
everywhere!

That's it, prepare
to disappear!

Uh-oh . . .

I'll never be able to fix all of this!

Hmm . . .

Eat my dust!

Wahooo!

Phooooffff!

See, no pencil can mess with me.

Perfectly clean . . .

Hey!